An Aesop's Fable
Retold by Pat Mora
Illustrated by José Ortega

 GoodYearBooks

Where is water hiding
on this hot, hot day?

3

Is it on the mountain? No, no, no.

4

Crow sees water hiding
on this hot, hot day.

Can he reach
the water?
No, no,
no.

Crow knows what to do.

Agua, agua, agua.

9

Crow finds pebbles
on this hot, hot day.

Una, dos, tres.
One, two, three.

11

Crow adds pebbles
on this hot, hot day.

Una. Can he drink
the water?
No, no, no.

13

Dos. Can he drink the water?
No, no, no.

15

Tres. Can he drink the water?
Sí, sí, sí.

Agua, agua, agua.